TELL THE TRUTH, B.B. WOLF

written by
JUDY SIERRA

illustrated by
J. OTTO SEIBOLD

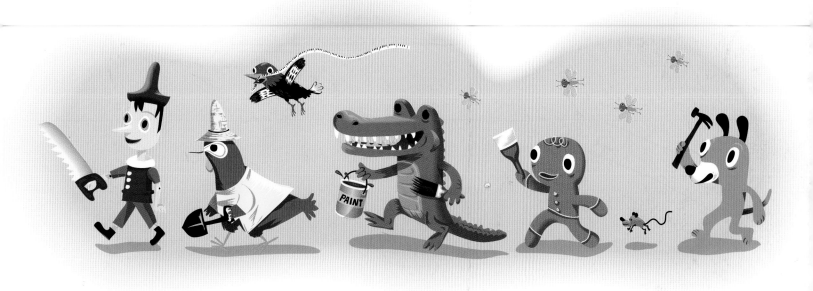

ALFRED A. KNOPF NEW YORK

Saturday was Fix-It-Up Day at the Villain Villa. The Big Bad Wolf and his chums were sawing and hammering and painting.

"Quiet!" shouted B.B. Wolf. "I have to answer my phone."

"Hello," said B.B. Wolf. "Sure. When? Today? Okay. Bye."

"What's the matter?" asked the crocodile.

"Miss Wonderly invited me to the library. She wants me to tell the story of how I met the three little pigs."

The troll knew "The Three Little Pigs" by heart.

"You wanted to eat those little piggies, didn't you?" cackled the witch.

"Put a spin on it," Rumpelstiltskin suggested. "Tell it your own way."

"Give it a happy ending," advised the crocodile. "Everyone expects a happy ending these days."

"I'll try," said B.B. Wolf, and he hurried to change into his best clothes.

At the library, Miss Wonderly led B.B. Wolf to a cozy chair in the story corner. B.B. Wolf started off with a song.

"Wrong!" squeaked a little voice.
"Your middle name is B-A-D."

B.B. Wolf growled. He began again,

HARD LUCK ALWAYS FOLLOWS ME,
♫ AND **TROUBLE** IS My MIDDLE NAME.
ANY TIME THERE IS **A CRIME**, ♫♫
♪ I'M THE **ONE** TO GET THE BLAME!

"I was gathering flowers one morning, and I picked a big dandelion puff. I blew on it—*whoo!*—and made a wish. Just then I heard someone shout, 'You blew my house down!' There, in the middle of a messy pile of straw, stood an angry little piggie. He started chasing me."

"Tell the truth, B.B. Wolf!"
oinked someone in the back of the library.

"Who's telling this story anyway?" B.B. Wolf asked. "All of a sudden, I smelled smoke. I followed my nose and found another little piggie playing with matches next to a pile of sticks. The sticks were on fire, so I blew on them as hard as I could—to put out the flames, you understand. Was the piggie grateful? No. He charged toward me."

"Isn't that wolf's snout getting longer?" asked Pinocchio.
"I think it is. I think it is," said the Little Engine.

"Okay, um, er, maybe it was the other way around. Anyway, I ran until I collapsed in front of a little brick house. I was tired and thirsty, so I banged on the door and begged, 'Please let me come in!' From inside the house, a piggie voice answered, 'Climb up on the roof and slide down my chinny-chin-chimney.'"

"No one is falling for your story," cracked Humpty Dumpty.

"It's a cooked-up, half-baked tale," snapped the Gingerbread Boy.

B.B. Wolf let out a dismal huff and a small, sad puff. "I didn't tell the truth," he groaned. "The truth is so embarrassing, and what's important is that I've changed. Really I have."

The three pigs stomped their trotters. "Apologize right now!" they demanded.

B.B. Wolf took a deep breath. "I'm s-s-s . . .

I'm s-s-s . . . I'm s-s-s . . .

Oh, I can't say it!"

"So I guess I'll have to sing it."

ONCE I
AND I
NOW I'M
LITTLE

WAS WILD AND WOOLLY,
ACTED LIKE A BULLY. 🎵🎶
BEGGING ON MY KNEES.
PIGS, FORGIVE ME, PLEASE!

"Well," said the first little pig, "I guess we could forgive you."

"It did happen a long time ago," said the second little pig.

"But your middle name is still Bad," added the third little pig.

"Goodness gracious!" exclaimed B.B. Wolf.
"I need a new middle name, don't I?"
He snagged a dictionary from the library shelf
and pawed through the pages.

"That's it!" said the wolf. "From this day forward, I am the one and only Big Bodacious Benevolent Bookish Wolf. In fact, I'll borrow some books right now."

"Toodle-oo!" he called to the three pigs. "See you in a few weeks!"

The wolf hurried home. He read, and thought, and planned, and drew lots of pictures.

"Those piggies would love their very own mud wallow," commented the crocodile.

"Why not trim the house with gingerbread," the witch suggested.

He and his chums went to work. In no time at all, the house was finished.

PRIVATE
MUD WALLOW
KEEP OUT!

"Friends," said the former menace, "it's not enough for me to say I'm sorry. I have to prove it and repair my reputation. Here is your very own piggyback mansion."

"Thank you!" squealed the three pigs.
And they began to sing,

THE WOLF WAS
MEAN AND VICIOUS.
HE THOUGHT PIGGIES
WERE DELICIOUS.
THEN HE LIED
and TOLD A STORY
THAT WAS WRONG,
AND HE WAS SORRY.
NOW HE'S CHANGED.
HE'S NOT PRETENDING.
THAT'S A VERY
Happy Ending!

Visit us on the Web! www.randomhouse.com/kids

Educators and librarians, for a variety of teaching tools, visit us at
www.randomhouse.com/teachers

Library of Congress Cataloging-in-Publication Data
Sierra, Judy.
Tell the truth, B.B. Wolf / by Judy Sierra ; illustrated by J.otto Seibold. — 1st ed.
p. cm.
Summary: When Big Bad Wolf, who now lives at the Villain Villa Retirement Residence, is invited to tell his story at the library, he faces the truth about what he did to the three little pigs and decides to make amends.
ISBN 978-0-375-85620-4 (trade) — ISBN 978-0-375-95620-1 (lib. bdg.)
[1. Honesty—Fiction. 2. Characters in literature—Fiction. 3. Wolves—Fiction.] I. Seibold, J.otto, ill. II. Title.
PZ7.S5773Te 2010
[E]—dc22
2009030778

The illustrations in this book were created using Adobe Illustrator.

MANUFACTURED IN MALAYSIA
August 2010
10 9 8 7 6 5 4 3 2 1
First Edition

Random House Children's Books supports the First Amendment and celebrates the right to read.